Disney
PUPPY for HANUKKAH

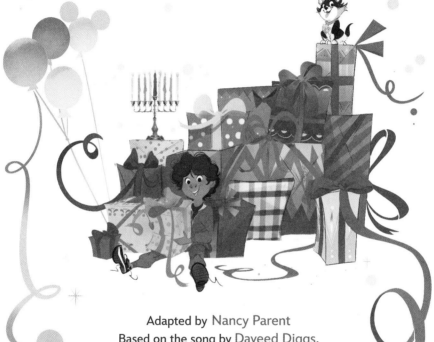

Adapted by Nancy Parent
Based on the song by Daveed Diggs,
William Hutson, and Jonathan Snipes
Illustrated by the Disney Storybook Art Team
Designed by Megan Youngquist

🎀 **A GOLDEN BOOK • NEW YORK**

Copyright © 2022 Disney Enterprises, Inc. All rights reserved. Published in the United States by Golden Books, an imprint of Random House Children's Books, a division of Penguin Random House LLC, 1745 Broadway, New York, NY 10019, and in Canada by Penguin Random House Canada Limited, Toronto, in conjunction with Disney Enterprises, Inc. Golden Books, A Golden Book, A Little Golden Book, the G colophon, and the distinctive gold spine are registered trademarks of Penguin Random House LLC.

rhcbooks.com
ISBN 978-0-7364-4340-1 (trade) — ISBN 978-0-7364-4341-8 (ebook)
Printed in the United States of America
10 9 8 7 6 5 4 3 2 1

Hanukkah is my favorite holiday!
I love **celebrating** every year.

Most holidays last just one day—
but **Hanukkah is special.**
It has eight days of . . .

latkes, dreidels, candles, menorahs, music,

family, and presents!

That's right, eight nights—*it's the Festival of Lights.*
We go hard for a week with a plus one.
So you all keep stressing, be good, learn lessons,
Because Hanukkah is the best **fun**!

Some kids write **lists** for their
   Christmas **gifts**,
And they send them off
   to their Santas.
But I don't trip off a list
   for the gift I'll get,
Because I've got **eight chances!**

And you know what I want, huh?
I want a puppy for Hanukkah!
(Bark if you're here, pup!)

On Hanukkah, we light candles and eat special
foods. Try some potato pancakes called **latkes**!
They go great with sour cream and applesauce.
Then we use the **shamash candle** in the middle
to light the **menorah** and say the Hanukkah blessing.

Pass that shamash candle; let's get the flame started.
By the way, have you got a present for me?
Is it what I wanted?

Hanukkah even has a **dreidel game** that you play with gold coins. Spin the top and see where it lands. **Nun, gimel, hei, shin!** "Gimel" gets you everything, "hei" gives you half, "shin" means to put two in, and "nun" gets you nothing.

But win or lose, I know I'll get some presents. Don't forget about the presents!

I'm going to get just what I wanted, yeah—
*I'm going to get a **puppy for Hanukkah!***

*Okay, **first night** and I'm feeling **right**.*
Mama came with a gift-wrapped box.

It doesn't **bark**, doesn't **bite**,
Doesn't cry when I shake it.
So I'm pretty sure it's just socks.

(But you never know—miracles happen. . . .)

And Hanukkah is a time to celebrate miracles!
Hundreds of years ago, **a little bit of oil** lit
ancient lamps that lasted for eight whole nights!
That's why we light candles and cook with oil.

But I'm hoping for a different kind of miracle
this year. . . .

I'm going to get what I want, yeah—
I want a puppy for Hanukkah!

The *lights keep burning*
  and the nights just pass.
The menorah is now covered up with wax.
I thought it was obvious; I didn't want to ask.
But will tonight be the night I get my puppy
  at last?
It's **all I ever wanted**, yeah.
Just a puppy for Hanukkah.

My feet are warm and my body is cozy.
The hats and the mittens and
   the umbrella are totally great!
Love it all—I'm the **King of Style**.
But there's one thing I've been wanting all this while.

Wait! Wait, is that . . . Could it be?
It's . . . Oh, oh my gosh!

*You're everything I ever
wanted, bruh.*
**You're my puppy
for Hanukkah!**

I'm gonna name you **Monica**!
It might be a weird name for a dog,
But it rhymes with **Hanukkah**.

I got my puppy
for Hanukkah!

Happy Festival of Lights

from me and my

Hanukkah puppy!

31901068662289